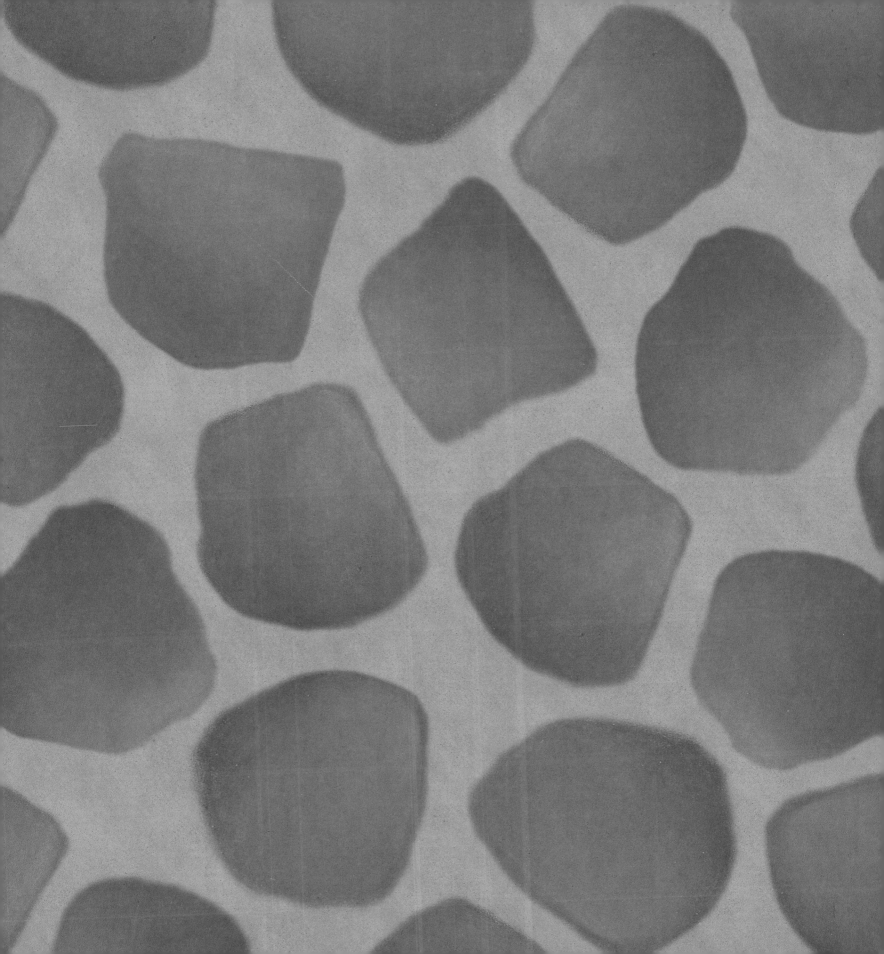

Gilda and Friends

Lucky

An orphan leopard
cub who has the
worst luck

Pepin

A persistent
penguin who loves
his family

Marvin

A silly little
marmoset who is
afraid of heights

Ernest

A young elephant who is
very afraid of mice

Gilda

A friendly giraffe who
loves melons and parties

Zander

A caring,
wise zebra who looks
out for his friends

Leonardo

An adventurous little
lion cub who likes to
go exploring

Papaya

A lovable panda who
eats a lot of bamboo

Turnip

A spirited young
turtle who loves an
adventure

We hope you enjoy the many adventures of Gilda and Friends. Our goal was to maintain the spirit of the original French-language story while adapting it to the Picture Window Books' format. Thank you to the original publisher, author, and illustrator for allowing Picture Window Books to make this series available to a new audience.

Editor: Jacqueline A. Wolfe
Page Production: Tracy Kaehler
Creative Director: Keith Griffin
Editorial Director: Carol Jones
Managing Editor: Catherine Neitge

First American edition published in 2006 by
Picture Window Books
5115 Excelsior Boulevard
Suite 232
Minneapolis, MN 55416
877-845-8392
www.picturewindowbooks.com

First published in Canada in 2000 by
Les éditions Héritage inc.
300 Arran Street
Saint Lambert, Quebec
Canada J4R 1K5

Printed in the United States of America.

Library of Congress Cataloging-in-Publication Data
Papineau, Lucie.
Gilda the giraffe and marvin the marmoset / by Lucie Papineau ; illustrated by Marisol Sarrazin.
p. cm. "Gilda the giraffe."
Summary: Marvin the marmoset resents being the object of ridicule by his family and friends, but when they put on a circus, he knows he must conquer his fear of heights in order to gain their respect.
ISBN 1-4048-1516-3 (hardcover)
[1. Marmosets—Fiction. 2. Monkeys—Fiction. 3. Animals—Fiction. 4. Fear—Fiction. 5. Circus—Fiction.]
I. Sarrazin, Marisol, 1965— ill. II. Title.
PZ7.P2115Giko 2005
[E]—dc22   2005011297

Gilda the Giraffe
and
Marvin the Marmoset

by Lucie Papineau
illustrated by Marisol Sarrazin
story adapted by Michael Dahl

PICTURE WINDOW BOOKS
Minneapolis, Minnesota

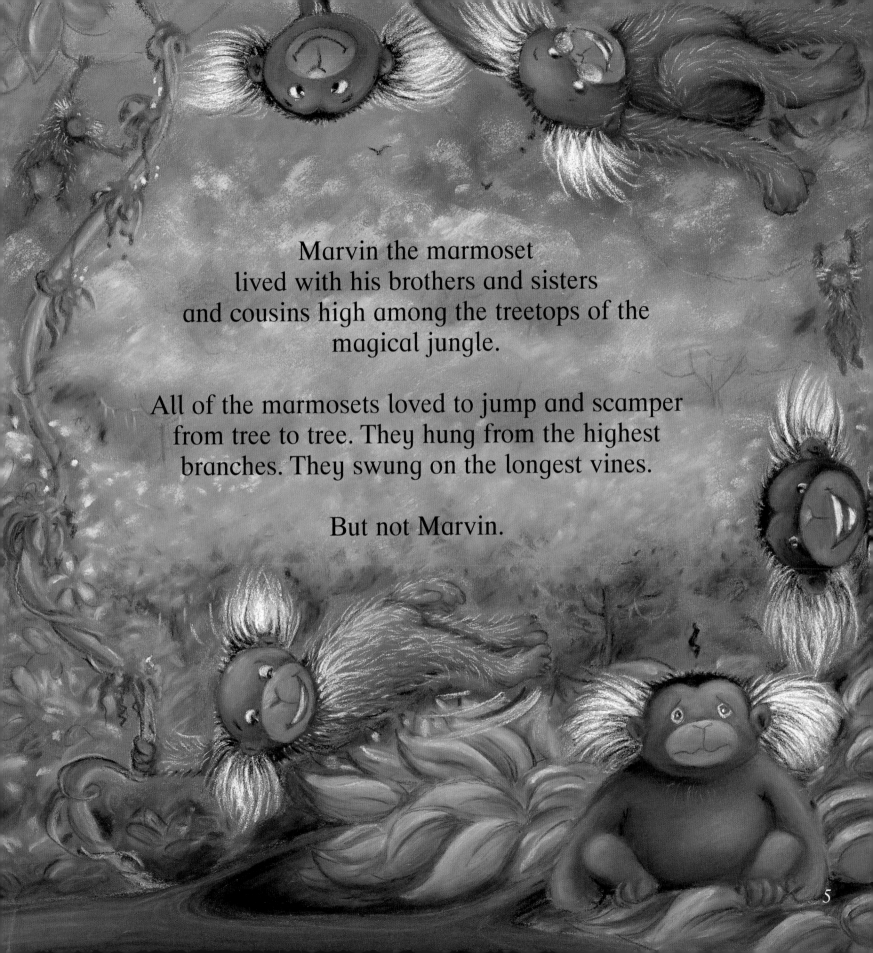

Marvin the marmoset
lived with his brothers and sisters
and cousins high among the treetops of the
magical jungle.

All of the marmosets loved to jump and scamper
from tree to tree. They hung from the highest
branches. They swung on the longest vines.

But not Marvin.

Marvin was afraid of heights.

All of his brothers and sisters and cousins made fun of him. "Marvin is too scared to climb," they teased.

6

Marvin pretended that he did not care. But, inside, he wished he could climb up high and play like everyone else.

Gilda the giraffe had a plan to help Marvin.

She called all of her friends together. "We are going to put on a circus," she said. And she showed them a small blue tent with banners all around it.

"We can't fit inside that little tent," said Ernest the elephant.

"Of course not," said Gilda. "This is a model of what our big circus tent will look like."

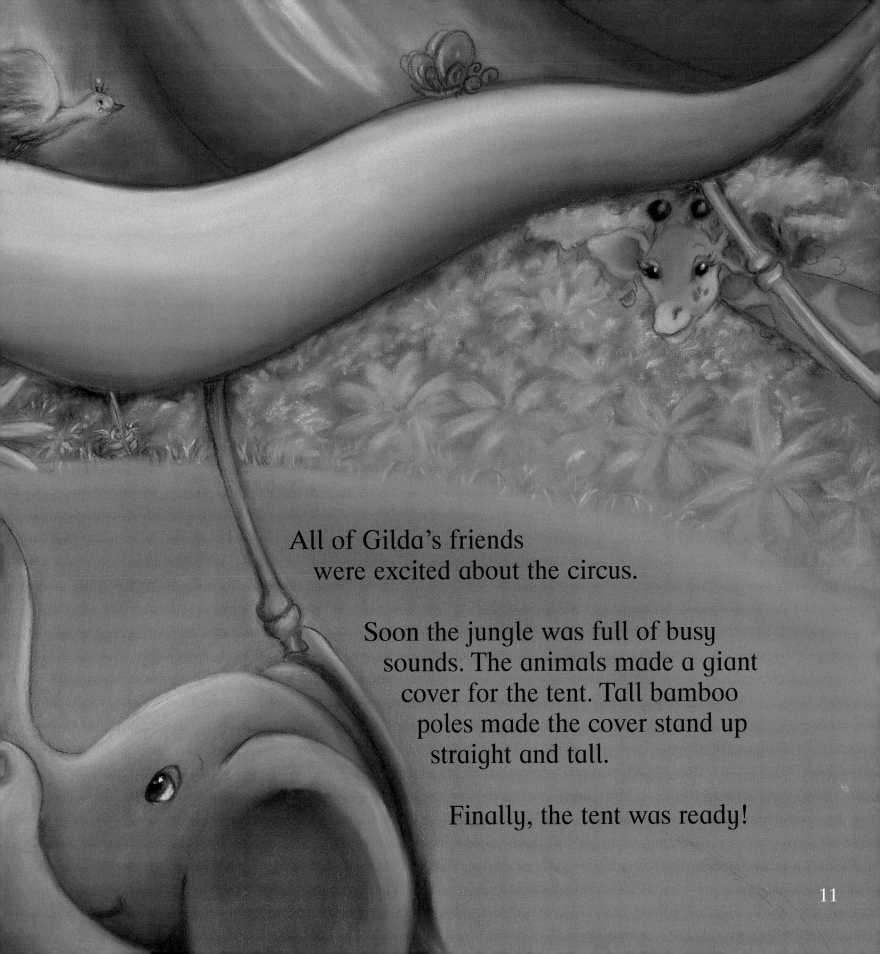

All of Gilda's friends
were excited about the circus.

Soon the jungle was full of busy
sounds. The animals made a giant
cover for the tent. Tall bamboo
poles made the cover stand up
straight and tall.

Finally, the tent was ready!

"What's next?" asked the animals.

"Now, we'll all work on our circus acts," said Gilda.

"I'll be the acrobat," said Ernest.

"We already have two acrobats," replied Gilda. "And I think they will do a magnificent job. We'll find something else very exciting for you, Ernest."

13

Marvin sat alone on the lowest branch of the smallest tree in the jungle. He could hear his animal friends busy working. He could hear his brothers and sisters and cousins laughing up in the trees.

Suddenly, Marvin felt a tug on his arm. It was Kiki the koala. "Hurry, Marvin," said Kiki. "We need you for our circus!"

"You need me?" asked Marvin.

"Yes," said the koala. "We need another acrobat to perform in the circus tent. Hurry! We have to practice!"

Marvin followed Kiki inside the giant circus tent.

"I can't climb way up there," said Marvin.

16

Then he watched as Kiki, who had quickly put on her costume, climbed up a tall ladder. Up and up she climbed, higher and higher. Marvin felt scared just looking at her.

"Watch me, Marvin," said Kiki, as she did a funny trick on the tightrope. Before he knew it, Marvin was laughing. He laughed so hard he no longer felt afraid.

18

The big night
finally arrived. The
show was about to begin!

Trumpets blew and drums
rolled. The ringmaster
stepped into the spotlight.

"Announcing our first
act. Ernest the elephant as ..."

"... the Mouse Tamer!"

The elephants in the audience all squealed with fear.
They gasped and carefully watched Ernest.

"How does he do it?" they wondered as they cheered.

"BRAVO! BRAVO!"

20

More and more amazing acts filled the
crowded tent. Animals sang and juggled.
They told silly jokes. Gilda and her
friends flew, danced, and
whirled like the wind.

It was time for the last act of the evening.

The ringmaster roared, "Announcing Kiki the Clown and Marvin the Magnificent!"

Marvin felt butterflies in his stomach.
He followed Kiki into the ring.

BoOM! He tripped.

The whole audience burst
into laughter.

The laughter felt good. It was different from the laughter of his brothers and sisters and cousins. The audience was not making fun of him. They were having a good time! The butterflies in Marvin's stomach disappeared.

The marmosets in the crowd were amazed by Marvin. "Will he climb up that tall ladder?" they asked.

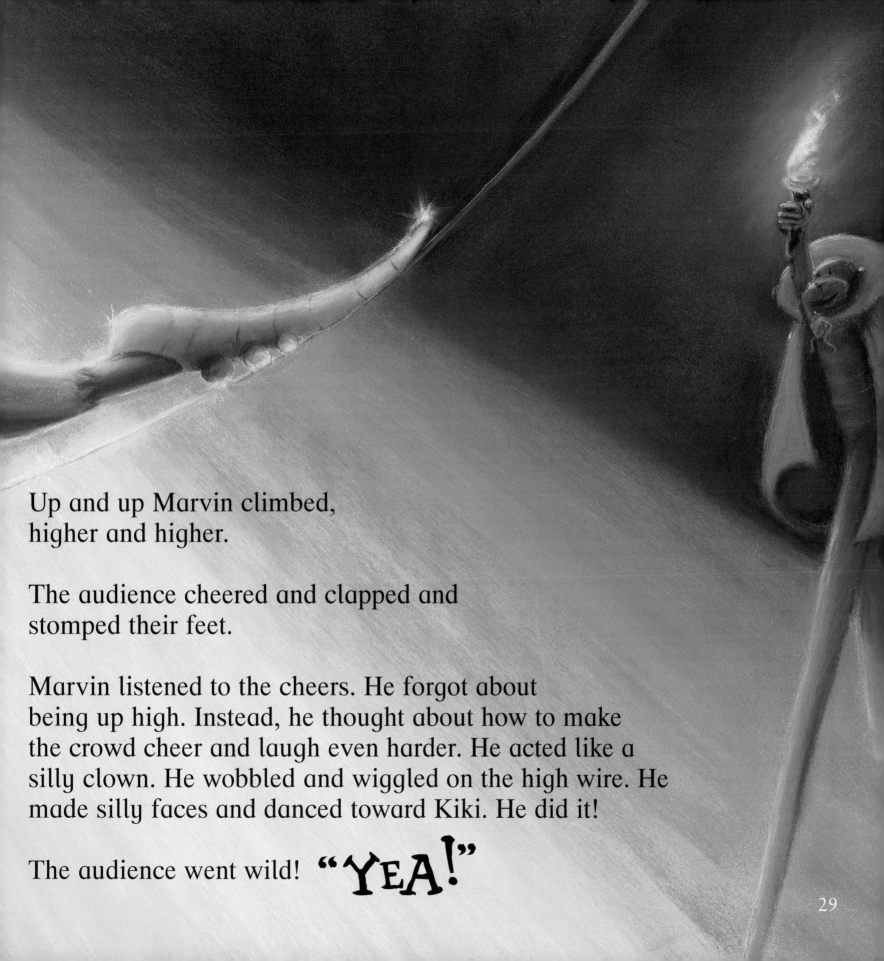

Up and up Marvin climbed,
higher and higher.

The audience cheered and clapped and
stomped their feet.

Marvin listened to the cheers. He forgot about
being up high. Instead, he thought about how to make
the crowd cheer and laugh even harder. He acted like a
silly clown. He wobbled and wiggled on the high wire. He
made silly faces and danced toward Kiki. He did it!

The audience went wild! "YEA!"

"And now for the Grand Parade!" shouted the ringmaster.

The circus acts were over, but the celebration was just beginning.

Marvin led the other animals out of the circus tent. He could hardly wait until tomorrow so he could perform his act again. This time, he would try it high in the treetops of the jungle.

31

Fun facts about Gilda's friends ...

- Marmosets are one of the smallest kinds of monkeys. Most are only 1 foot (.305 meters) long!

- Marmosets live in the tallest trees of tropical rainforests. Most marmosets like to run and hop on large tree branches.

- Some marmosets bite into tree trunks and then hop away for a few hours. They come back and eat the sticky sap that has dripped from the bite mark.

- In large marmoset families, some members do nothing all day but carry and take care of the young. Some families have as many as 15 members.

Go on more adventures with Gilda the Giraffe:

On the Web

FactHound offers a safe, fun way to find Internet sites related to this book. All of the sites on FactHound have been researched by our staff.

Here's how:

1. Visit www.facthound.com

2. Type in this special code for age-appropriate sites: 1404815163

3. Click on the FETCH IT button.

Your trusty FactHound will fetch the best sites for you!

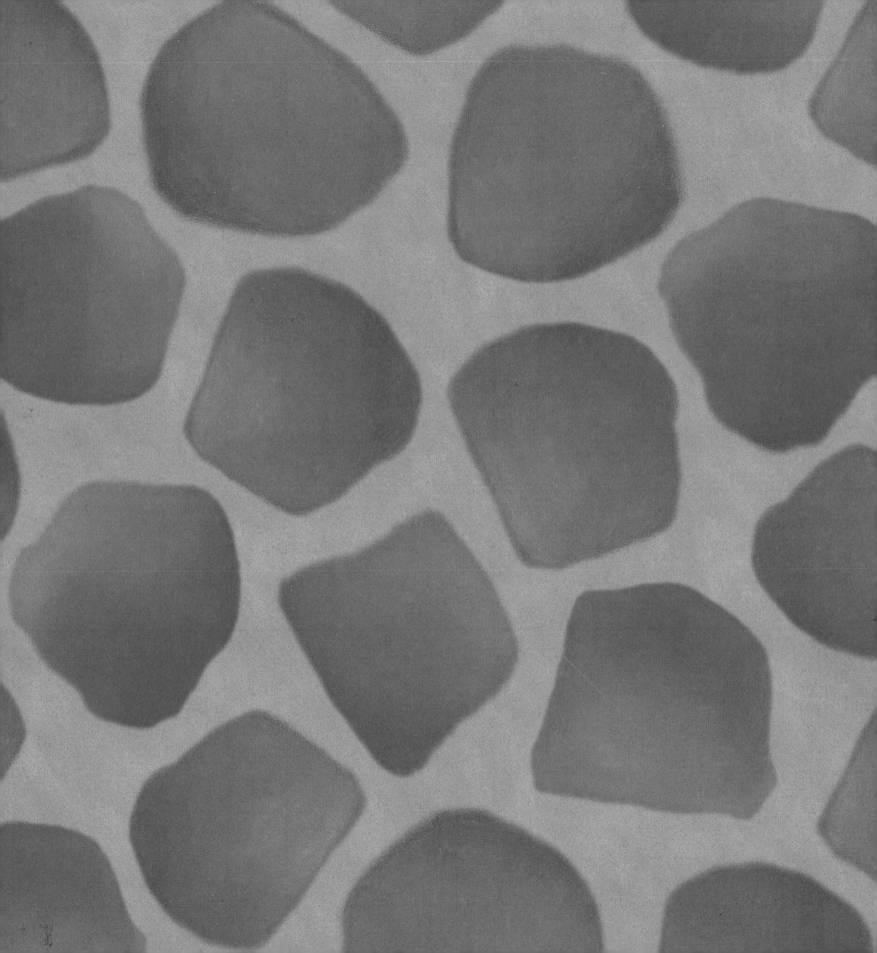